"The Baseball Game Is On!"

Welcome baseball fans, kids, parents, gramm...
Who will win this big game and be this year...

The Eagles can throw and catch the ball, with such precision.
The red, white and blue can hit the ball, with their great vision.

**EAGLES
3**

**SHARKS
4**

The Sharks play to get three outs, and eliminate their prey.
The white, yellow and red, score runs, and dominate the play.

The score is 4 runs to 3 for the Sharks, they are winning.
Let's watch the game, the Sharks are at bat, in the 9th inning.

Have fun watching the action, all eyes are on the play.
And practice your reading, to surprise someone today.

Make use of those red letters and blue words, a handy guide.
All the letters have sounds, that make words, along each side.

Practice early reading skills using the special page format.
- see the Literacy Guide chart on page 54 -
4 Building Blocks Of Reading - With Suggested Reading Skills Activities

Sports Action Kids Books - Book 3
ISBN-978-1-7771741-7-0

sportsactionbooks@gmail.com

Copyright ©️ Coach Craig B.Ed. 2020

"Go! Eagles! Soar-High!", some fans cheer up in the stands.

A a
B b
C c
D d
E e
F f
G g
H h
I i
J j
K k
L l
M m
N n
O o
P p
Q q
R r
S s
T t
U u
V v
W w
X x
Y y
Z z

The Eagles are ready to play defense, and get three outs.

"Go! Sharks-On-The-Hunt!",
others shout, clapping their hands.

ready

play

defense

three

outs

batter

runner

set

let's

play

ball

umpire

shouts

The batter and runner are set,
"Play ball," the umpire shouts.

A a
B b
C c
D d
E e
F f
G g
H h
I i
J j
K k
L l
M m
N n
O o
P p
Q q
R r
S s
T t
U u
V v
W w
X x
Y y
Z z

The pitcher checks the runner,
he goes into his wind up.

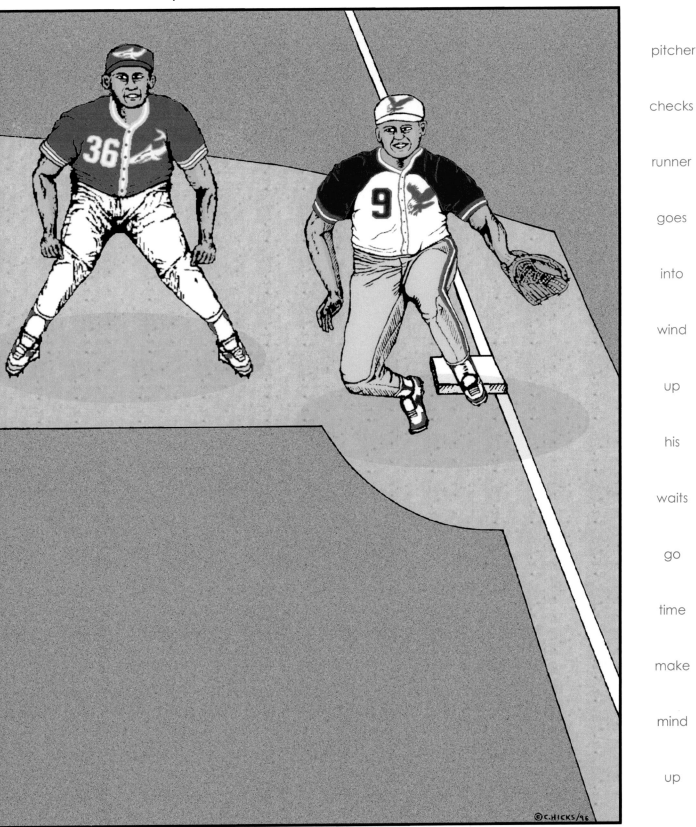

pitcher

checks

runner

goes

into

wind

up

his

waits

go

time

make

mind

up

The runner waits. Will he go?
It's time to make his mind up.

A a
B b
C c
D d
E e
F f
G g
H h
I i
J j
K k
L l
M m
N n
O o
P p
Q q
R r
S s
T t
U u
V v
W w
X x
Y y
Z z

The pitcher turns. The Shark goes! He takes off with great speed.

6

pitcher

turns

Shark

takes

off

great

speed

steps

pitch

quickly

took

good

lead

The pitcher steps to throw,
as the Shark took a good lead.

A a
B b
C c
D d
E e
F f
G g
H h
I i
J j
K k
L l
M m
N n
O o
P p
Q q
R r
S s
T t
U u
V v
W w
X x
Y y
Z z

A swing and a miss! The catcher stands up, to make a throw.

swing

miss

catcher

stands

up

make

throw

aims

second

base

shark

runner

go

He aims for second base, as he sees the Shark runner go.

A a
B b
C c
D d
E e
F f
G g
H h
I i
J j
K k
L l
M m
N n
O o
P p
Q q
R r
S s
T t
U u
V v
W w
X x
Y y
Z z

The Shark looks for second base,
he runs and slides for the bag.

Shark

looks

second

base

slides

bag

ump

shouts

OUT!

Eagle

ball

puts

tag

The ump calls, "OUT!" The Eagle
with the ball, puts on the tag.

A a
B b
C c
D d
E e
F f
G g
H h
I i
J j
K k
L l
M m
N n
O o
P p
Q q
R r
S s
T t
U u
V v
W w
X x
Y y
Z z

The pitcher throws a fast ball,
and the batter likes it.

pitcher

throws

fast

ball

batter

likes

it

Pop!

Shark

ball

swings

bat

strikes

it

"Pop!" goes the ball, as the Shark swings his bat and strikes it.

A a
B b
C c
D d
E e
F f
G g
H h
I i
J j
K k
L l
M m
N n
O o
P p
Q q
R r
S s
T t
U u
V v
W w
X x
Y y
Z z

©C.HICKS/96

The ball is thrown in, as the Shark takes off with a quick burst.

thrown

ball

Shark

takes

off

quick

burst

He

base

beats

calls

ump

safe

first

He beats the ball to the base,
so the ump calls, "Safe at first!"

A a
B b
C c
D d
E e
F f
G g
H h
I i
J j
K k
L l
M m
N n
O o
P p
Q q
R r
S s
T t
U u
V v
W w
X x
Y y
Z z

The pitcher throws, the runner sprints for second and hustles!

throws

pitcher

runner

sprints

second

hustles

Shark

hits

swinging

hard

bat

with

muscles

A Shark hits the ball, swinging his bat hard with his muscles!

A a
B b
C c
D d
E e
F f
G g
H h
I i
J j
K k
L l
M m
N n
O o
P p
Q q
R r
S s
T t
U u
V v
W w
X x
Y y
Z z

© C.HICKS/96

The Eagle shortstop scoops up the ball, and whips it across.

Eagle

shortstop

scoops

ball

whips

across

second

base

foot

on

snags

quick

toss

With his foot on second base,
an Eagle snags the quick toss.

EAGLES
3

STRIKES
1

BALLS
1

The Shark slides, as the Eagle jumps up to avoid a crash.

Shark

slides

Eagle

jumps

avoid

crash

OUT

ump

fires

ball

the

quick

flash

©C.HICKS/96

"OUT!" calls the ump. He fires the ball as quick as a flash.

A a
B b
C c
D d
E e
F f
G g
H h
I i
J j
K k
L l
M m
N n
O o
P p
Q q
R r
S s
T t
U u
V v
W w
X x
Y y
Z z

The first baseman catches the ball, to complete the relay.

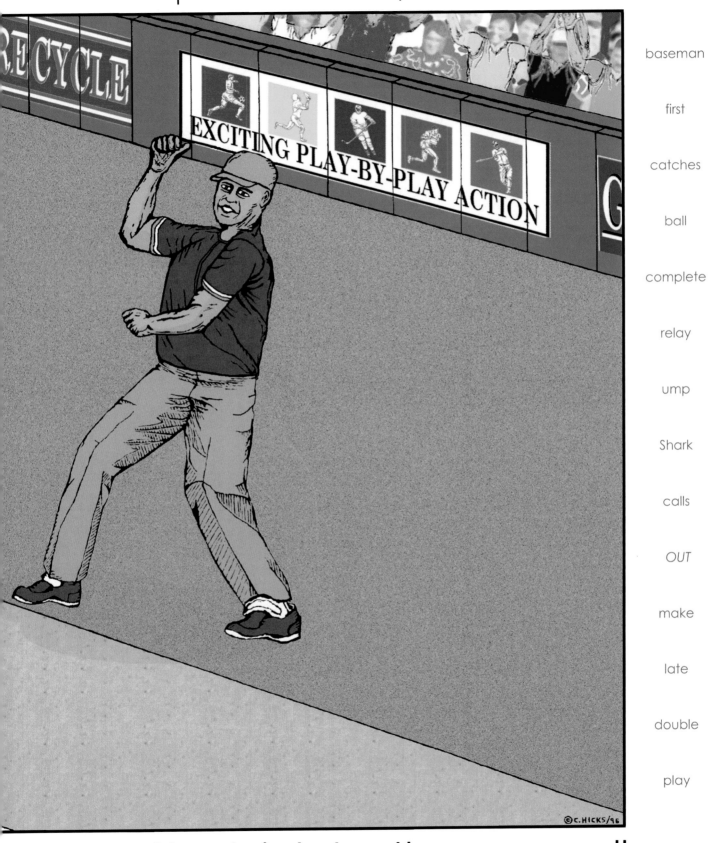

RECYCLE

EXCITING PLAY-BY-PLAY ACTION

G

baseman

first

catches

ball

complete

relay

ump

Shark

calls

OUT

make

late

double

play

©C.HICKS/96

The Shark is late, the ump calls, "*OUT !*," to make a double play.

"Go! Eagles! Soar-High!"
sing out some fans, all united.

A   a
B   b
C   c
D   d
E   e
F   f
G   g
H   h
I   i
J   j
K   k
L   l
M   m
N   n
O   o
P   p
Q   q
R   r
S   s
T   t
U   u
V   v
W   w
X   x
Y   y
Z   z

The Eagles come to bat, the Shark whips the ball from his mound.

"Go! Sharks-On-The-Hunt!",
chant other fans, all excited.

Eagles

come

bat

Shark

ball

mound

whips

from

batter

turns

quick

rips

right

around

The Eagle batter turns quick,
and rips his bat right around.

EAGLES	STRIKES	BALLS
3	1	1

A a
B b
C c
D d
E e
F f
G g
H h
I i
J j
K k
L l
M m
N n
O o
P p
Q q
R r
S s
T t
U u
V v
W w
X x
Y y
Z z

Oh! A well hit ball, so high to the out-field and deep!

Oh

well

hit

ball

so

high

out-field

deep

Shark

Wow

wall

catches

big

leap

Wow! The Shark at the wall,
catches it with a big leap!

A a
B b
C c
D d
E e
F f
G g
H h
I i
J j
K k
L l
M m
N n
O o
P p
Q q
R r
S s
T t
U u
V v
W w
X x
Y y
Z z

©C.HICKS/96

The pitcher throws a curve ball, aiming for his catcher's mitt.

pitcher

curve

throws

aiming

catcher's

mitt

ball

off

bat

swings

getting

good

hit

The ball flies off the bat as he swings, getting a good hit.

A a
B b
C c
D d
E e
F f
G g
H h
I i
J j
K k
L l
M m
N n
O o
P p
Q q
R r
S s
T t
U u
V v
W w
X x
Y y
Z z

The Eagle sprints to second, giving the Sharks some trouble.

sprints

Eagle

second

giving

some

trouble

fielder

whips

ball

in

him

stopping

double

The fielder whips the ball in, stopping him at a double.

A a
B b
C c
D d
E e
F f
G g
H h
I i
J j
K k
L l
M m
N n
O o
P p
Q q
R r
S s
T t
U u
V v
W w
X x
Y y
Z z

The Shark pitcher whips a fast ball,
he brings in the heat.

pitcher

whips

the

fast

ball

brings

heat

runner

goes

batter

swings

digs

cleat

The runner goes, the batter swings and digs in his cleat.

"Go! Eagles! Soar-High!",
some fans cheer up in the stands.

A a
B b
C c
D d
E e
F f
G g
H h
I i
J j
K k
L l
M m
N n
O o
P p
Q q
R r
S s
T t
U u
V v
W w
X x
Y y
Z z

©C.HICKS/96

The ball rockets past the pitcher,
he reaches from his mound.

"Go! Sharks-On-The-Hunt!", others shout, clapping their hands.

ball

rockets

past

pitcher

reaches

from

mound

shortstop

dives

ball

bounces

off

ground

The shortstop dives for the ball, as it bounces off the ground.

A a
B b
C c
D d
E e
F f
G g
H h
I i
J j
K k
L l
M m
N n
O o
P p
Q q
R r
S s
T t
U u
V v
W w
X x
Y y
Z z

©C.HICKS/96

The runner slides for home,
the catcher is set at the plate.

runner

slides

home

catcher

set

plate

Safe!

tie

game

ball

tag

come

too

late

"Safe!" The Eagles tie the game,
the ball and tag came too late.

A a
B b
C c
D d
E e
F f
G g
H h
I i
J j
K k
L l
M m
N n
O o
P p
Q q
R r
S s
T t
U u
V v
W w
X x
Y y
Z z

Next run wins! The batter checks the ball speed and location.

NINTH INNING VICTORY

EXCITING PLAY-BY

wow

next

run

wins

batter

checks

speed

location

pitcher

threw

curve

ball

daring

determination

The pitcher throws his curve ball, with daring determination.

A a
B b
C c
D d
E e
F f
G g
H h
I i
J j
K k
L l
M m
N n
O o
P p
Q q
R r
S s
T t
U u
V v
W w
X x
Y y
Z z

The Eagle swings fast, the fans jump to a thunderous crack!

Eagle

swings

hard

fans

jump

thunderous

crack

bat

meets

ball

crushes

with

tremendous

whack

His bat meets the ball, crushing it with a tremendous whack!

EAGLES
4

STRIKES	BALLS
1	1

A a
B b
C c
D d
E e
F f
G g
H h
I i
J j
K k
L l
M m
N n
O o
P p
Q q
R r
S s
T t
U u
V v
W w
X x
Y y
Z z

The ball flies to the wall, as the batter swings with all of his might.

42

ball

flies

wall

with

batter

swings

might

catcher

frozen

everyone

turns

watch

ball's

flight

The catcher is frozen, as everyone turns to watch the ball's flight.

A a
B b
C c
D d
E e
F f
G g
H h
I i
J j
K k
L l
M m
N n
O o
P p
Q q
R r
S s
T t
U u
V v
W w
X x
Y y
Z z

A Shark jumps stretching for the ball,
to stop a game winning run.

jumps

stretching

ball

stop

game

winning

run

sails

above

glove

high

ninth

inning

done

But it sails high above his glove,
and the ninth inning is done.

Oh! Yeah! Wow! Alright!, shout some fans, they start an uproar!

A a
B b
C c
D d
E e
F f
G g
H h
I i
J j
K k
L l
M m
N n
O o
P p
Q q
R r
S s
T t
U u
V v
W w
X x
Y y
Z z

©C.HICKS/96

Oh baby! It's gone! A home run! He runs around all the bases.

Oh! No! Geez! Oh-man!, pout other fans, they cheer no more!

Oh

baby

gone

home run

runs

around

bases

Eagles

win

Sharks

tried

stand

frowns

faces

The Eagles win! The Sharks tried, but stand with frowns on their faces.

Wow! What fun and excitement for the fans who came.
The Sharks and Eagles played an awesome game.

The players fought hard with no energy to spare.
In the heat of the battle they always played fair.

EAGLES

5

SHARKS

4

The players now walk about and greet one another.
They reach to fist pump, showing respect for each other.

Yes, winning the championship is a sensation.
And, playing with sportsmanship wins admiration.

___

Grown ups! Let's help the kids learn good reading skills.
Like athletes have coaches for good training drills.

The 4 building blocks of reading are shown in a chart.
Try some of the tips to help make the kids really smart.

Practice early reading skills using the special page format.
- see the Literacy Guide chart on page 54 -
4 Building Blocks Of Reading - With Suggested Reading Skills Activities

Baseball Player Positions

Offensive Players: When a team has its turn at bat all of their players become offensive players, each player becomes a hitter getting a turn at bat. Each batter stands in the batter's box and tries to get on base by hitting the baseball when it is pitched to them.

Defensive Players: When a team is not at bat nine players make up the defensive team. Each player plays a specific position and has an important role in helping to get outs and to prevent the other team from scoring runs. The nine players are pitcher, catcher, first base, second base, shortstop, third base, right field, center field, and left field.

Pitcher: The player who pitches the ball to each batter, by throwing the ball over or near home plate to the catcher. He plays his position from the pitching mound in the center of the baseball infield. Pitchers will try to throw strikes and also try to throw the baseball to the catcher in different locations to make the batter swing and miss the ball. They will throw fast balls, curve balls and change the speed of the ball to try and fool the batter with each pitch. Pitchers also play defense around the mound when a baseball is hit.

Catcher: The defensive player whose position is directly behind home plate. He catches each pitch thrown by the pitcher. The catcher gives the pitcher a target with his glove and will give signals to the pitcher on where to pitch the ball and what kind of pitch to throw. Catchers also play defense around home plate when the ball is hit.

First Baseman: The player who plays near first base. He is responsible for making an out by touching first base after he catches the ball before an opposing runner tries to touch first base. They also play defense around first base when the ball is hit.

Second Baseman: The player who plays near second base. He is responsible for making an out by touching second base after he catches the ball before an opposing runner tries to touch second base. They also play defense around second base when the ball is hit.

Third Baseman: The player who plays near third base. He is responsible for making an out by touching third base after he catches the ball before an opposing runner tries to touch third base. They also play defense around third base when the ball is hit.

Shortstop: The player who plays between second base and third base. They play defense in the area between second and third base when the ball is hit. They will also help the second baseman cover second base and make outs by touching second base when they have possession of the ball.

OutField: The right fielder, center fielder, and left fielder are three players that play in the outfield. They are responsible for catching fly balls as well as running down ground balls that make it through the infield. They then throw the ball into the infield to make outs and stop runs from being scored.

The fans are so excited, on the edge of their seats!

A a
B b
C c
D d
E e
F f
G g
H h
I i
J j
K k
L l
M m
N n
O o
P p
Q q
R r
S s
T t
U u
V v
W w
X x
Y y
Z z

The Eagle fielders are all set as their pitcher takes aim.

And they are nervous, no time for cell phone calls or tweets!

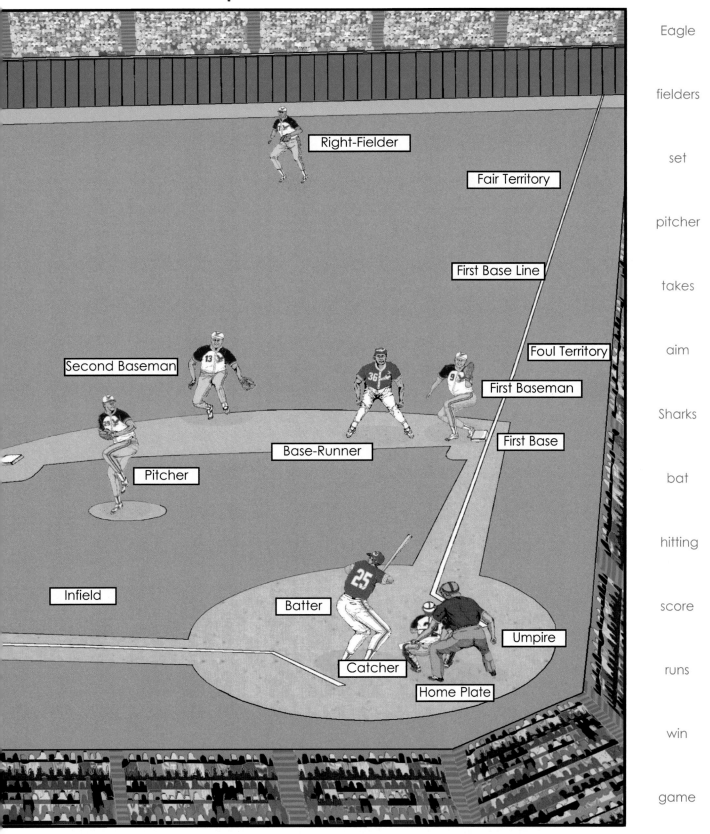

Eagle

fielders

set

pitcher

takes

aim

Sharks

bat

hitting

score

runs

win

game

The Sharks are at bat, hitting to score runs and win the game.

Baseball Glossary

Ball: A pitch which does not pass through the strike zone and is not swung at by the batter (four balls thrown to a batter allows him to get on base).

Base: The four points of the baseball diamond, first, second and third bases and home plate. A base runner must touch each base in order to score a run.

Batter: The offensive player who is positioned in the batter's box set to hit the ball (hitter).

Batter's Box: Area on both sides of home plate where the batter stands during his time at bat.

Bottom: The last (second) half of an inning (example: bottom of the ninth inning).

Catch: When a fielder gains possession of the ball in his glove or hand before it touches the ground and firmly holds it.

Change-up: A pitch thrown by the pitcher at a slower rate of speed, trying to fool the hitter.

Curve Ball: A pitch thrown by the pitcher that will drop down or curve to one side; the pitcher is attempting to fool the hitter (they will swing where the ball will not be).

Defense: The team currently in the field.

Double: A play in which the batter runs and makes it safely to second base without stopping after hitting the ball.

Double Play: A defensive play in which two offensive players are put out as a result of one play of continuous action; the ball is caught and thrown between fielders and basemen.

Fast Ball: A pitch thrown very fast. The pitcher attempts to make the batter swing and miss the ball by overpowering the hitter with a very fast moving ball (brings in the heat).

Fielder: One of the nine defensive players in the field, including pitcher, catcher, first baseman, second baseman, third baseman, shortstop, left fielder, center fielder and right fielder.

Fly Ball: A ball which goes high in the air when batted (pop fly).

Foul Ball: A batted ball that lands on foul territory.

Ground Ball: A batted ball which rolls along the ground (grounder).

Home Plate: The base over which an offensive player bats, and to which he must return after touching all three bases in order to score a run. Where the pitcher aims each pitch and where the catcher plays his position.

Home Run: A play in which the batter makes it safely around all bases and back to home plate without stopping after hitting the ball.

Home Team: The team on whose field the game is played.

Infield: The diamond-shaped portion of the playing field bordered by the four bases.

Infielder: A fielder who plays in the infield, includes the pitcher, catcher, first baseman, second baseman, third baseman, and shortstop.

Inning: A period of time where both teams get a turn at bat while the other team plays defense. Each team is allowed three outs to try and score as many runs as they can each inning.

Line Drive: A ball which is batted directly to a fielder without touching the ground.

Offense: The team that is currently at bat trying to get hits and to score runs.

Out: A decision by the umpire that a player who is trying for a base is not entitled to that base. An out occurs when:
1. A fly ball that is caught by a fielder.
2. When the ball is thrown to a base before a player runs to that base.
3. Three strikes have been called against a batter.

Outfield: The portion of the playing field that extends beyond the infield and is bordered by the first and third baselines.

Outfielder: A fielder who occupies a position in the outfield.

Pitch: When the ball is thrown by the pitcher to the batter (curve ball, fast ball, change-up).

Run: A score made when an offensive player (batter) has ran and touched all the bases and returned to home plate.

Runner: An offensive player who is advancing toward, touching or returning to any base (an offensive player on base).

Safe: A decision by the umpire that a runner who is trying for a base has not been tagged or forced out, and is therefore entitled to that base (is not out, is safe).

Single: A play in which the batter safely makes it to first base.

Strike: A pitch, which:1. Is swung at by the batter and missed;
2. Is not swung at, but the ball passes through the strike zone; (Umpire call)
3. Is fouled by the batter when he has less than two strikes;
(three strikes thrown to a batter and the batter is out)

Strike Zone: An area directly over home plate, from between the batter's knees to the area just below his chest (the umpire decides if a pitch is ruled a strike or a ball by using this zone).

Tag: The action of a fielder in touching a base with his body while holding the ball, or touching a runner with the ball, or with his hand or glove while holding the ball.

Throw: The act of propelling the ball toward another teammate. A pitch is not a throw.

Top: The first (beginning) half of an inning (example; the top of the ninth inning).

Triple: A play in which the batter makes it safely to third base without stopping.

Literacy Guide Chart

Practice early reading skills using the special page format.

-The special page format is designed for children to practice key skills in their reading development.
-The story text is in black, and the alphabet letters in blue on the left, with story words in red on the right.
-This is a handy reference to practice some early reading skills, before, during or after reading the story.

4 Building Blocks Of Reading - With Suggested Reading Skills Activities

-The chart below highlights 4 specific skills that are key building blocks required to produce a new reader.
Use their current ability as a guide to focus on the appropriate skills to practice.

1
Oral Language Development

Speaking aloud and expressing ideas and thoughts builds oral language skills and provides an essential foundation for the development of reading.

Suggested Activities

- look through the story letting the child talk and tell about the pictures using their own words

- encourage, listen and actively respond to the child's own words, thoughts and ideas

-prompt for more oral discussion and detail with questions and rephrasing their words and ideas

-take turns talking about the action and what the players and fans might be feeling, thinking and saying

2
Letter and Sound Recognition

An essential pre-reading skill is recognizing all the letters (upper and lower case) of the alphabet and the sounds that they make.

Suggested Activities

- together point to each blue letter, name and make the sound of each letter in the alphabet

- explain letters have a lower case (small) symbol and upper case (big) symbol

- name a letter, the sound it makes and then have your child point to it (take turns making it a fun game)

- identify a letter and see if it can be found in a red word on the left and in the story (letters make words)

3
Building Word Vocabulary

An important reading skill development is the ability to visually identify words, to recognize the grouping of letters and to remember the word meaning.

Suggested Activities

- point to and say a red word, name each letter and their sounds that group together making each word

- point to and read a red word and then let your child find it in the story sentence (take turns making it a game)

- take turns pointing to and reading aloud each red word from the top to bottom in order

- point to a red word, have your child say the word and explain its meaning (make a sentence with the word)

4
Reading Fluency and Comprehension

Developing the ability to read words accurately and understand their meaning at the same time produces a fluent and competent reader.

Suggested Activities

- read the story together, develop a rhythm and use the rhyme to create and model a natural reading fluency

-ask questions about the action and events to check for memory and understanding

- discuss the thinking, emotions and feelings of the many players and spectators watching the game

- talk about team work, fair-play and sportsmanship, allowing your child to express their feelings and ideas

Find a good balance between working with a child's current abilities and challenging them to learn!
Support literacy development!

Sports Action Kids Books - Book 3
ISBN-978-1-7771741-7-0

sportsactionbooks@gmail.com

Made in the USA
Middletown, DE
22 December 2020

29926219R00031